TOOLS RULE!

ATHENEUM BOOKS FOR YOUNG READERS • An imprint of Simon & Schuster Children's Publishing Division • 1230 Avenue of the Americas, New York, New York 10020 • • Interior design by Aaron Meshon and Ann Bobco • Jacket design by Ann Bobco • The text for this book is hand-lettered. • Manufactured in China • 0114 SCP • First Edition • 10 9 8 7 6 5 4 3 2 1 • Library of Congress Cataloging-in-Publication Data • Meshon, Aaron, author, illustrator. • Tools rule! / by Aaron Meshon. — 1st ed. • p. cm • Summary: In a messy yard, a team of tools gets organized, then spends a busy day building a shed. • ISBN 978-1-4424-9601-9 (hardcover) • ISBN 978-1-4424-9602-6 (eBook) • [1. Tools—Fiction.] • I. Title. • PZ7.M5492Too 2014 • [E]—dc23 • 2013009361

Aaron used many tools to build this book! The story was written using the keyboard on a MacBook Pro laptop. Sketching the layout and characters came next, using a Staedtler 2B pencil. Aaron then drew darker, more finalized, lines on Staples recycled copy paper, using a Faber-Castell PITT Artist Brush Tip Pen. Sixty-plus pages of text and final line drawings were then scanned using a Fujitsu ScanSnap into his MacBook Pro's hard drive, and then colored digitally in Photoshop. The wood texture used for Workbench was a scan of Aaron's kitchen cutting board! During most of the building of this book, Chubu, a twenty-seven-pound French bulldog, was on Aaron's lap, helping out.

atheneum
Atheneum Books for Young Readers
New York London Toronto Sydney New Delhi

In a messy yard...

a busy day begins.

OKAY, CREW!!!
Who's ready to build?
zzzzzz
zzzzzzzzz

Where is everyone?
Vise, we're all scattered.
What should we do?

My advice? Let's get a grip on things. We need to organize! Take a roll call!
Write on!

Wrench?
CLICK! CLICK! Here!
Hammer?
BANG! BANG! Here!

Workbench?
Workbench?
Ummm...
You are standing on me!
HERE!

Saw?
Saw?
Saw?
zzzzzzz
I saw Saw just a minute ago!

Brush?
Tape measure?
They are missing too!
Drill? DRILL?
Flashlight?
Level? LEVEL?

Where IS everyone?

AW, NUTS!
They're still lying around!

Ladder
Cat
Level
Drill
Mower
Nails
Saw
What a mess! Calling all tools...

Wagon
Tape
Neighbor's dog
Screwdriver
Nuts and Bolts
Flashlight
Awl
Brushes and Paint
Wheelbarrow
Wood
to the workbench one and all. Awl, that means you too!

Let's work together
We will have a place
Yes!
Let's stick together!

to build a toolshed!
to rest our heads!
OKAY!
Sealed!

Please build it around ME!
Because he's too heavy to move.

CONSTRUCTION TIME IS HERE!
ZZZ

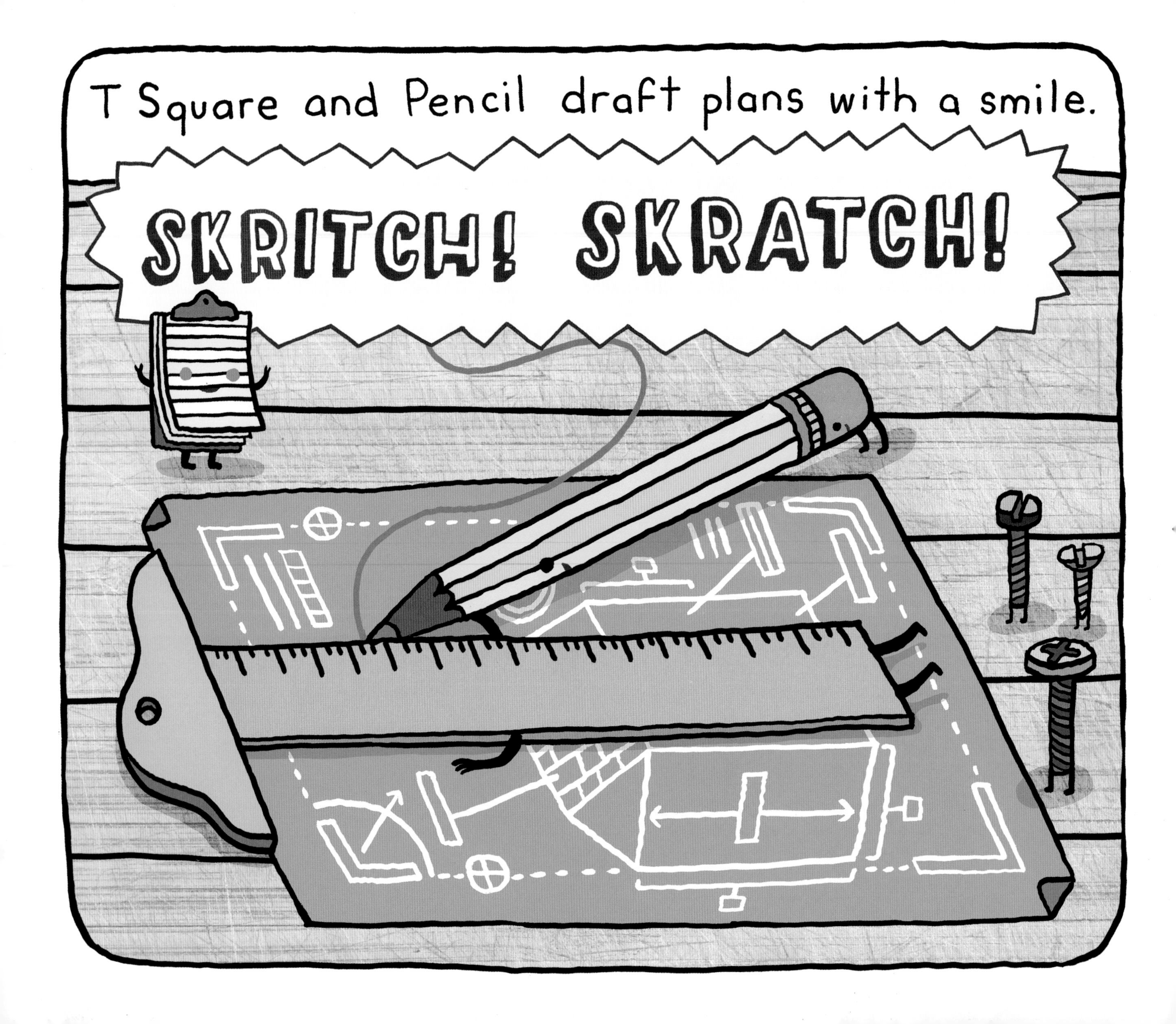
T Square and Pencil draft plans with a smile.
SKRITCH! SKRATCH!

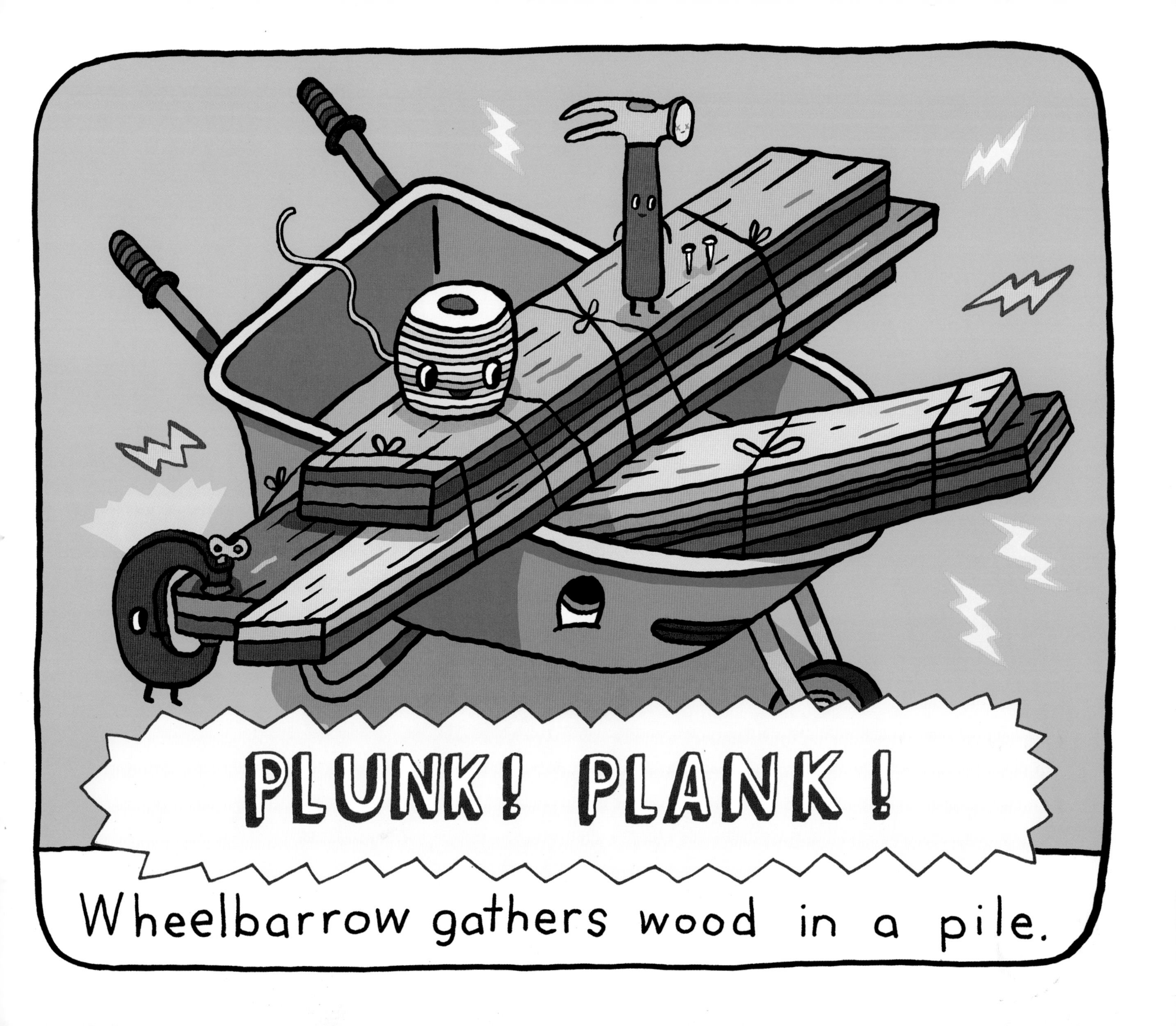

Wheelbarrow gathers wood in a pile.

Saw saws Wood.
VRIP!
VRIP!
VRIP!

Drill drills Screws.
ZIP!
ZIP!
ZIP!

The frame is up and standing tall.

Hey, Nails, it's time to build a wall!
OK! ouch! OK! OK! ouch! OK! OK! ouch!

Is everything straight?
Level inspects.
GUGGLE!
GUGGLE!
Glad I checked.

Glue glues on Roof Tiles.
GLIP! GLAP! GLOP!
Brush brushes Paint.
SWISH! SWASH! SLOP!

Pail pours.
It's concrete for the floor!
Smooth move!

Wrench works.
Let's attach the door!

The shed is
Now we can finally

finished and it's the best.
get some rest!
Looks sharp!

In an organized shed . . .

a busy day ends.

Great hanging out with you all, but now I'm BEAT!
Tucked in!

Yawn.
And I'm full!
ZZZZZ
Stretch!

LIGHTS OUT!
Good night,
everyone.

Sweet dreams, Drill!
'Night, Nails!
Sleep tight, Tape!
Don't snore,
Screwdriver!

ZZZ...ZZZ...ZZZ...
CLUNKZZZ
CLONKZZ
ZZZ!
BUBBLEZZ!
GUGGULZZ!
GLOPZ
Pourzzz...zzz...zzz
ZZZ
CLANKZ!
DRILZZZZ!
BANGZZ...
BANGZZ...
DROPZZZ...
ZZZ
ZZZ
zzz...zzz...